Acting Edition

C000121034

Mom, How Did You Meet the Beatles?

A True Story of London in the 1960s

by Adrienne Kennedy
and Adam P. Kennedy

FOR PRODUCTION INQUIRIES

UNITED STATES AND CANADA
info@concordtheatricals.com
1-866-979-0447

UNITED KINGDOM AND EUROPE
licensing@concordtheatricals.co.uk
020-7054-7298

Each title is subject to availability from Concord Theatricals Corp.,
depending upon country of performance. Please be aware that *MOM,
HOW DID YOU MEET THE BEATLES?* may not be licensed by
Concord Theatricals Corp. in your territory. Professional and amateur
producers should contact the nearest Concord Theatricals Corp. office
or licensing partner to verify availability.

THE PUBLIC THEATER

OSKAR EUSTIS
Artistic Director

MARA MANUS
Executive Director

Presents

MOM. HOW DID YOU MEET THE BEATLES?

By ADAM P. KENNEDY and ADRIENNE KENNEDY
Directed by PETER DUBOIS

with
WILLIAM DEMERITT, BRENDA PRESSLEY

Scenic and Costume Design	ALEXANDER DODGE
Lighting Design	MICHAEL CHYBOWSKI
Sound Design	WALTER TRARBACH
Production Stage Manager	ELIZABETH MILLER

General Manager
NICKI GENOVESE

Associate Artistic Director
MANDY HACKETT

Associate Producer
JENNY GERSTEN

Director of
the Musical
Theater Initiative
TED SPERLING

Resident
Director
PETER DUBOIS

Director of
Development
CASEY REITZ

Director of
Marketing
ILENE ROSEN

Director of
Communications
CANDI ADAMS

Casting
JORDAN THALER
HEIDI GRIFFITHS

Director of Production
RUTH E. STERNBERG

The PUBLIC LAB is made possible through the generous support of the Andrew W. Mellon Foundation. Additional support for the PUBLIC LAB is provided by the Ford Foundation, The Booth Ferris Foundation, and HBO, Inc.

The LuEsther T. Mertz Charitable Trust provides leadership support for The Public's year-round activities.

Time Warner is the Supporting Sponsor of The Public's 2007-2008 season. Bank of America is the Lead Sponsor of Shakespeare in the Park. Major support is provided by The Doris Duke Charitable Foundation, The New York State Music Fund, The Shubert Foundation, The Carnegie Corporation of New York, The Susan Stein Shiva Foundation, The George T. Delacorte Fund at the New York Community Trust–Fund for Performances at the Delacorte Theater in Central Park, and by Warren Spector and Margaret Whitton. Pepsi is the official beverage sponsor of The Public Theater.

Additional generous support is provided by Debra and Leon Black, The Horace W. Goldsmith Foundation, The Starr Foundation, The Harold and Mimi Steinberg Charitable Trust, Titan Worldwide, and The New York Times. Public support is provided by the New York City Department of Cultural Affairs; the New York State Council on the Arts, a state agency; and the National Endowment for the Arts, an independent federal agency. Cultural Partners include WNYC and the Manhattan Chamber of Commerce. Pickle Press is the official printer, and Continental Airlines is the official airline of The Public Theater.

MUSIC AND THIRD-PARTY MATERIALS USE NOTE

IMPORTANT BILLING AND CREDIT REQUIREMENTS

MUSIC AND THIRD-PARTY MATERIALS USE NOTE

Licensees are solely responsible for obtaining formal written permission from copyright owners to use copyrighted music and/or other copyrighted third-party materials (e.g. artworks, logos) in the performance of this play and are strongly cautioned to do so. If no such permission is obtained by the licensee, then the licensee must use only original music and materials that the licensee owns and controls. Licensees are solely responsible and liable for clearances of all third-party copyrighted materials, including without limitation music, and shall indemnify the copyright owners of the play(s) and their licensing agent, Concord Theatricals Corp., against any costs, expenses, losses and liabilities arising from the use of such copyrighted third-party materials by licensees. For music, please contact the appropriate music licensing authority in your territory for the rights to any incidental music.

IMPORTANT BILLING AND CREDIT REQUIREMENTS

If you have obtained performance rights to this title, please refer to your licensing agreement for important billing and credit requirements.

THE PUBLIC THEATER

OSKAR EUSTIS
Artistic Director

MARA MANUS
Executive Director

Presents

MOM, HOW DID YOU MEET THE BEATLES?

By ADAM P. KENNEDY and ADRIENNE KENNEDY
Directed by PETER DUBOIS

with
WILLIAM DEMERITT, BRENDA PRESSLEY

Scenic and Costume Design	ALEXANDER DODGE
Lighting Design	MICHAEL CHYBOWSKI
Sound Design	WALTER TRARBACH
Production Stage Manager	ELIZABETH MILLER

General Manager
NICKI GENOVESE

Associate Artistic Director
MANDY HACKETT

Associate Producer
JENNY GERSTEN

Director of
the Musical
Theater Initiative
TED SPERLING

Resident
Director
PETER DUBOIS

Director of
Development
CASEY REITZ

Director of
Marketing
ILENE ROSEN

Director of
Communications
CANDI ADAMS

Casting
JORDAN THALER
HEIDI GRIFFITHS

Director of Production
RUTH E. STERNBERG

The PUBLIC LAB is made possible through the generous support of the Andrew W. Mellon Foundation.
Additional support for the PUBLIC LAB is provided by the Ford Foundation, The Booth Ferris Foundation,
and HBO, Inc.

The LuEsther T. Mertz Charitable Trust provides leadership support for The Public's
year-round activities.

Time Warner is the Supporting Sponsor of The Public's 2007-2008 season. Bank of America is the Lead
Sponsor of Shakespeare in the Park. Major support is provided by The Doris Duke Charitable Foundation,
The New York State Music Fund, The Shubert Foundation, The Carnegie Corporation of New York, The
Susan Stein Shiva Foundation, The George T. Delacorte Fund at the New York Community Trust—Fund
for Performances at the Delacorte Theater in Central Park, and by Warren Spector and Margaret Whitton.
Pepsi is the official beverage sponsor of The Public Theater.

Additional generous support is provided by Debra and Leon Black, The Horace W. Goldsmith Foundation,
The Starr Foundation, The Harold and Mimi Steinberg Charitable Trust, Titan Worldwide, and The New
York Times. Public support is provided by the New York City Department of Cultural Affairs; the New York
State Council on the Arts, a state agency; and the National Endowment for the Arts, an independent federal
agency. Cultural Partners include WNYC and the Manhattan Chamber of Commerce. Pickle Press is the
official printer, and Continental Airlines is the official airline of The Public Theater.

CHARACTERS

ADRIENNE KENNEDY – The Adrienne character is often hestitant, emotional, joyous and sad. The conversation with her son is the *first time* she has spoken about her time in London during the 1960s.

ADAM KENNEDY – Throughout the play, the Adam character is curious as to events he's heard something about. This is the *first time* he's heard the story from his mother.

AUTHOR'S NOTES

In London, in the 1960s, there was music everywhere. The Beatles, The Stones, The Supremes, James Brown, Aretha, Jimi Hendrix, music from the musical *Hair*, Dylan, etc.

Specific 1960s songs were used in the Public Theater production. I have indicated who the artists were so that the music can approximate these sounds.

Also regarding the Public Theater production: we used specific London scenes–pictures of The National Theatre, Primrose Hill, Maida Vale, Adrienne and Adam on Chalcot Crescent, The Royal Court, and the National Theatre.

*(**ADRIENNE KENNEDY** enters center stage and remains there. **ADAM KENNEDY** is seated close to the wings [partially seen].*

***ADRIENNE** wears a pretty dress—silver was popular—and perhaps ballerina shoes. **ADAM** wears dark trousers and a white shirt.*

*Throughout the play, **ADRIENNE** looks at the audience. There are only a few moments where she glances back at the actor behind her.*

*Behind **ADRIENNE** are scenes of London during the 1960s.)*

ADAM KENNEDY. **How did you come to work with the Beatles?**

ADRIENNE KENNEDY. Joe *[Joseph C. Kennedy]* and I were separated and somehow you and I ended up living on Bedford Street for about eight months and I was miserable. I didn't see a way out. Gillian Walker came to see a production of *The Owl Answers* at the Theatre de Lys. She was a New York career girl with all this energy and enthusiasm and this love for *Funnyhouse*. She had already seen *Funnyhouse*. She told me she worked for Ted Mann's theatre Circle-In-the Square. She was Ted's assistant, but she was far more. She really was co-producer. I knew Ted Mann because I had studied at Circle-In-the Square...*Funnyhouse*...that's where *Funnyhouse* had its very first workshop production at Circle-In-the Square on Bleecker Street.

She said, "Maybe we could commission you to write a play." Bedford Street was only a stone's throw from Bleecker Street. So I walked around there. You were in school in kindergarten.

I walked around there and went up to see Ted. He said

7

I'd like to commission you to write a play. So...that just sounded so good to me. He said, "What do you want to write?" Well, a couple of years before, Joedy had given me a book about the Beatles...John Lennon's nonsense books. I was always crazy about this book. It's a little blue book. It has a photograph of John Lennon on the cover and these little nonsense verses. I was always just so taken with it. So I said I'd like to make a play of John Lennon's nonsense writings. I thought that really sounded great...maybe go to London and meet the Beatles or something. *(laughs)* It was crazy in a way, because I was in my mid-thirties. But...you know...that's what I said.

He said, "Well I know John Lennon's publisher. His name is Tom Maschler. I'll write to Tom Maschler and ask him...you know...maybe you could get permission to make a play out of John Lennon's nonsense book." He didn't say that's crazy or whatever. So Gillian wrote the letter, "a great idea," she said.

She wrote to Tom Maschler in London and Maschler... I think answered right away...and he said something like, "Tell her if she's ever in London to look me up." He said something like, "that sounds interesting. I can't make any promises, but tell her if she's ever in London to look me up."

Well I was a desperate person *(laughing)*...you know what I mean. And I thought I was going to get a Guggenheim. I was almost sure I was going to get a Guggenheim. And I'm stuck on Bedford Street. And there we were and I didn't know what I was going to do. So I said what I'll do, since I'm going to get a Guggenheim, I already had a Rockefeller Grant and, of course, Joe was giving me alimony...so, I'll take my little money and I'll go to London.

And...it was just a desperate move, a totally desperate move. I was walking down the street, on a Tuesday. We went to London on Thursday. And on Tuesday, I was walking down Bleecker Street…Gillian said we could spend the last night in her house at the Dakota, which turned out to be very strange, because that's where John Lennon was murdered.

I was walking down Bleecker Street and I saw Diana Sands. Diana Sands always regretted that by the time *Funnyhouse* reached Off Broadway she couldn't be in it. She was on Broadway in *The Owl and the Pussycat* with Alan Alda. Diana was the original *Sarah* in *Funnyhouse*. She said, "Adrienne, I've always felt so terrible about it…where are you going? She was going to Circle-In-the-Square too. She had an appointment with Ted Mann.

As we walked I told her I was going to London in a few days. She said, "I've just come back from London and I want to give you a list of people you can look up there." She'd been doing *The Owl and the Pussycat* in the West End.

She said where will you be the last night here? The… last night…was a Wednesday. I told her the Dakota at Gillian's. She came to the Dakota and brought a long list of all these people. I remember she told me to call Ricki Huston first because she had a child your age. So I had all these people in the theatre to look up.

With that list and this message from Tom Maschler, on the strength of that I pulled myself together and took us to London in search…of…something.

We stayed at the Dakota the last night. I've always that that was very strange. The Dakota, I don't know if you remember…the Dakota had some rooms…rooms up on the top floor that servants used to sleep in…babysitters and housekeepers. Some tenants had a room like that. Gillian's friends used to stay in that little room. They were enchanting little rooms. We stayed in that little room upstairs for our last night.

And then we set off…we left in the morning for London. And I remember being at JFK. It was November…something like November 27, 1966. It was November 26 or November 27. And you were so trusting. You were just…you know…I said, "Adam; we're going to London." And you were always just so trusting. And we're at the airport and I'm talking to you about going to London. And we got on a plane and went to London. We…I think had about four hundred dollars maybe five but no more. I didn't know. I just wanted to change my life.

Gillian had given me the name of what they called a "bed-sit." They didn't call them pensiones; they called them bed-sitters. A writer she knew lived in one in Earls Court. She told me to go there and ask form him. It would be a place to stay.

(London theme music begins playing.)

We arrived in London at about ten o'clock at night. And I went to this bed-sit and I asked for this writer. A woman said he wasn't there. And she was hostile… the woman who ran it. You could tell she was shocked that I was Black and that I was asking to stay in this bed-sit. I said, "Well, doesn't this writer live here?" She said, "He's not here." He's in Paris or something like that. "You can't stay here."

Gillian had another name written down…the Basil Street Hotel. I didn't know the Basil Street Hotel is one of the fanciest little hotels in London. So it's ten o'clock at night. We're trudging with our suitcases looking for a taxi.

(London theme music begins to fade.)

I don't know a soul in London. All I have is addresses, Diana Sands' theatre connections. So we go to the Basil Street Hotel at about eleven at night. And they were so nice. This beautiful little hotel. It's right around the corner from Harrods.

I'm sure by now it costs a fortune. And it had these enchanting little rooms with wall paper…

(Tea dance music begins playing.)

…like an Agatha Christie novel…Colonel so and so

came down for breakfast. They gave tea dances. We were only there about two weeks, but they gave tea dances in the afternoon and Colonel so and so is dancing with his wife. And they were so nice to us. I think they were nice to us because…*(pause)*…you didn't see many American Blacks in London. And I think people were just a little taken aback. I really do.

(Tea dance music begins to fade.)

I think I had the letter from Tom Maschler, but I'm not sure. But I certainly had his address, Bedford Square and the name of the publisher, Jonathan Cape. And I had Ricki Huston's address. The very next day I called Tom Maschler and I called Ricki Huston.

(Ricki's theme music should be in the realm of Jagger, Hendrix, Aretha, the Supremes.)

I had seen Ricki's picture many times…on the cover of *Life* magazine…in magazines skiing with John Huston…at home with John Huston. She answered the phone. I couldn't believe I was talking to her. She said, "Darling, I give teas on Sunday. You're a friend of Diana's. Please come by. Come by on Sunday."

I called Tom Maschler. He said he couldn't see me until that next week. We went to Ricki's on Sunday. The Hustons lived in Maida Vale No. 31 on the canal… Little Venice. The rooms were palatial and filled with art objects. She was very beautiful…with three beautiful children…Tony, Anjelica, Allegra. A governess lived with them. They seemed to like us. And they particularly liked you. I don't want to underestimate that. People were taken with you. I had you dressed up in this little blazer and shirt. It was very expensive. Not that it cost as much as Prince Charles…but it was expensive. When Joedy came from Sierra Leone they liked him too. Ricki put his picture on her dresser. So Ricki sort of took us on as her American friends…her Sundays at four.

(Ricki's music begins to fade.)

By the next Tuesday…I think it was the next Tuesday… I took you…Tom Maschler said he couldn't see me until like 5:00 pm. He said, "I'll see you at the end of the day." He said, "I want to tell you…I can't promise you anything except that you can come by." I said, "You told me, if ever I was in London, I could look you up." *(laughs)* He never dreamed that I was flying to London then. It was just a little crazy.

So we went…I came up from underground. His office was on the right, Bedford Square. We went in and I left you sitting in the little lobby. It was dark. It's December now…a week later *[after leaving New York]*. It's the first week in December and it's dark and cold. I went into his office. He turned out to be a young man about… twenty eight…dark-haired, intense.

He said, "What are you doing here in London?" I said I have a Rockefeller Grant and I'm probably going to get a Guggenheim and I'm just here for a little while. I told everyone that, I was just there for a couple of weeks. I told everybody that, because I really didn't know. I had already sent him twenty pages. I don't know when I did that. I think I did that from New York. I just sat down real quick and sent him twenty pages of the *Lennon Play*.

He said, "I can't give you money and I can't give you the rights to make a play out of John Lennon's *In His Own Write*. But what I will do, I will tell John. I will tell John about you." He said, "That's all I can promise you." He said, "But you will have to finish the whole thing, and I can't pay you." He said it was nice meeting me. So we left.

(Tea dance music begins playing.)

So we were there at the Basil Street Hotel. We went to Ricki's the next Sunday and that gave me a sense of security. Ricki was like that. She either embraced you or I guess she didn't pay any attention to you. But she embraced us.

…I remember that Christmas we went to the panto-mime Cinderella at the Palladium. Do you remember that?…

(Tea dance music out.)

We were still at the Basil Street Hotel. Then…an American couple, Ann and Carlton Colcord, had pro-duced *A Rat's Mass* in Rome. I had corresponded with them. They knew what I looked like from a photo I had sent them. They had lived in South American and now lived in Rome.

ADAM. And you had never met them?

ADRIENNE. I had never met them. We were standing on the corner facing Harrods…all these kinds of…I don't know…these weird occurrences. We were standing on the corner facing Harrods, starting to cross the street and go to the Basil Street Hotel, and this man was standing next to me. He said, "Aren't you Adrienne Kennedy?" And I said, "Why, yes." And he said, "Well, I'm Carlton Colcord."

(London theme music begins. It should be in the vein of The Byrds, music of the era.)

He said he too was staying at the Basil Street. He said, "Ann and I are thinking of moving to London. Ann's coming here in a few days, and she's going to stay at the Basil Street Hotel. We have two little children. In fact, we have a little boy who's Adam's age."

It had always been on my mind that we should go back to New York and I began to feel like we couldn't stay at the Basil Street Hotel. I began to feel like maybe we should go back to New York. But I'd given up that little horrible apartment on Bedford Street. So I couldn't go back.

The apartment we lived in before Joe and I sepa-rated, four hundred Central Park West had been so beautiful.

We had Ricki's teas and everybody was nice to us.

Then we stayed at a bedsitter on Queensgate Terrace. You walked out and there at the corner was Kensington Palace. I was excited…then Janet Miguell, Ricki's friend, who helped run the Leslie Waddington Art Gallery said, "You and Adam can stay with us for a while."

She lived in an apartment across from Olympia. We saw a boat show there once. The apartment was a kind of building I'd never seen…gigantic, red structure with large, wandering apartments. Janet and Gina *[Ricki's best friend]* lived there. Gina was a painter who later married an Olympic athlete. Large paintings were on the walls.

I kept working on the Lennon pages and working on the pages and working on the pages. Then I forgot about it. I said, "Maybe I should go back home." I called up the Guggenheim. I said, "I know you don't announce the Guggenheim until April first"…and this was January… "but do you think I'm going to get a Guggenheim?" A secretary said she did not generally give out that kind of information. But she said she would talk to the Foundation and find out. *(laughs)* I don't know why I did these kinds of things. Here I am in London *[in January]* and I need to know whether I'm going to get the Guggenheim in April. *(More laughter)* I don't know where I got that from. My mother would die. I mean I don't know where I got the nerve to do things like that.

Someone called me. "You are going to get a Guggenheim."

ADAM. So how much was that worth? How much was the Guggenheim?

ADRIENNE. It was eight thousand, five hundred dollars, which was a fortune back then. People lived on eight thousand, five hundred dollars. I knew it was enough money for us to live on for a year. Joe was giving me money each month. I had a Rockefeller grant. Rockefeller grants were three thousand, five hundred dollars. But I had spent quite a bit of the Rockefeller grant already.

We were just lucky. Now I felt we could stay in London. So I went out looking for apartments. You know there was this big racial thing in London. And there weren't many American Blacks…when I showed up people seemed a little…

ADAM. **When you say there was a big racial thing, what do you mean?**

ADRIENNE. People were very aware that you were not white. At that time a lot of West Indians were moving to London. You know there was a tradition of Africans living and going to school in England, Cambridge, Oxford, and University of London. But now the British thought too many West Indians were moving to London. It was very much in the air.

People would be surprised that I was Black. I would call first after seeing an apartment in The London Times. I didn't know what I was doing.

(Primrose Hill music begins. It is joyous.)

So Janet Miguell said, "Adrienne, I don't think you know how to find an apartment in London. I'll find you an apartment." She made a few phone calls. Then she said, "You should live up in Primrose Hill. A lot of Americans live up there. It's not expensive but it's beautiful. Some writers live there but it's still working class."

So I went up there in a taxi. It seemed far away. We went up this street; I think it's called Albert Road. There was the Zoo and Primrose Hill. Janet told me Karl Marx once walked there and Sylvia Path had lived on Chalcot Square. She had found an apartment for us. She said, "They're thrilled. I told them you're a Guggenheim Fellow. They have a pretty little apartment at the top of their house." I remember it was seventy pounds a month, which was about two hundred and ten dollars.

So we went there. They said you're a writer and a Guggenheim Fellow. They let us move in right away. It was on the corner, 39 Chalcot Crescent. You went up the stairs to the top floor of their house. It was a beautiful little living room, hallway, kitchen and a bedroom that faced a garden.

The day we moved to Primrose hill I got a phone call. "Hello Adrienne, this is James Earl Jones." We had met when Ellen Holy had introduced us backstage at a production of Macbeth that Joe Papp had done in Washington Square Park. I remembered his unusually intense brown eyes. "I'm in London and I don't know anyone."

My new friends all wanted to meet him. Ricki invited a group to her house. Jimmy was preparing to do a movie in France with the Burtons, a Graham Greene novel. His mention of the Burtons reminded me of my obsession with Elizabeth Taylor. "Jimmy, when you're making the movie with the Burtons, could you get me Elizabeth Taylor's autograph?" "I will," he said matter of factly. He came to London several times while filming the movie, once bringing with him a man who was writing a book on Africa. Finally at the end of the summer Jimmy came to London again. Would he be going back to France?

"The filming is over," he said. "Did you ever get Elizabeth Taylor's autograph?"

"No. I wanted to because I knew you really wanted it, but I felt funny asking her for an autograph."

(Primrose Hill music begins to fade.)

The man Jimmy had brought to visit was Alex Haley. He came up the stairs full of energy, carrying books under his arm. He sat on a gray silk couch and we talked about young marriages, which we both had experienced. He told me that he was writing a book that would trace his ancestors back to West Africa. Although I had been to West Africa with Joe for six months and knew it had changed my entire consciousness, I still laughed. The idea of a person tracing his family back that far was funny to me. "You shouldn't laugh," he said very genially, "in fact you should trace yours." I never forgot it.

After we'd been there for about four months, the family decided they didn't like having visitors in their house. It wasn't renovated. And when we went up the stairwell we passed by their upstairs rooms.

It was near July, the landlord said, "Mrs. Kennedy, there's a man down the street and he's stationed in Nigeria. They have two floors and they're for rent. It's only five pounds more than this and it's all furnished." And I'll never forget. I went down there and looked at it. "I called the agent for you and I told him you're an American, you're over here on a Guggenheim and he said he'll lease it to you for a year." So we took our suitcases and went to No. 35. And to me it was like Shangri-La. It was a beautiful two floors of a house with a garden, two baths, beautiful bedrooms. It was furnished very traditionally. There was a living room that faced the garden.

The dining room had a mantle piece, striped wallpaper and a big dark dining table with chairs. And the living room had a settee. It wasn't a couch, it was a settee. And striped gold wallpaper. Then you walked down three steps and there was a kitchen. It faced the garden. And you walked down about five or six more steps and there were two bedrooms, with two baths. Your room faced the garden. To me, it was like heaven.

I never heard from Tom Maschler. I had forgotten, really, about the Beatle thing. Anyway, Billie Allen had said to me, "You've got to call up Nan Lanier when you're in London." Well I had never called Nan Lanier.

Nan Lanier was Tennessee Williams' cousin. She's my

age. She was divorced…had been married to a minister in New York. I can't remember his name. Nan was one of the founders of the American Place Theatre. And Nan Lanier loved *Funnyhouse*. When I called her. She said, "Adrienne, I've been wondering how to find you." She said, "Billie told me that you're over here. Where do you live?" And I told her 35 Chalcot Crescent. And she said, "Well, we live right above you. We live in Hampstead. All you have to do is just walk up the hill and then turn the corner and there we are." By now it was summer. It was warm outside. So I took you and we walked up the hill…and there she was.

You see it was an atmosphere…She was an exile…She was divorced. She had children. All these people were running around her house. It was a huge house. You know, she's the rich American divorcee. You see there were so many people that were like me, people who were in London because London had this aura and they were coming to look for something.

She asked what I was doing. I told her I had these pages of a *Lennon Play* and that I had met once with Tom Maschler. And she said, "Oh, Adrienne. I can help you. Victor Spinetti. You know him. He was in both Beatle movies. *Help* and *Hard Day's Night.*" And this is just what she said, "He's my dearest friend and he knows the Beatles very well. I know he would love to work on a project like this." *(laughs)* And we had just walked up the hill to say hello to her. There was something in the air, Adam. There really was something in the air…

Nan went to the phone and called him. He lived near Baker Street. She said, "He can't come over right now. But he wants you to come down to the theatre to see him tomorrow. He's in *The Odd Couple* on Leicester Square." You know, the famous square where all the theatres are. You were in school. I don't think I took you, but I'm not sure.

So I went down to see Victor and he was excited. He said, "Nan says you have an adaptation of John Lennon's nonsense book. John is a friend of mine. What I'll do is I'll go out to"...I think they lived someplace called Weybridge... "I'll go out to Weybridge and talk to John. And I'll find out if he would like to work on something like this." I think he called John...he did! He called me up and he said, "I've called John and he's very interested in this." So Nan Lanier's all excited now. She calls to tell me that Victor's called up John and John is very interested.

In the meantime, mother had brought Joedy from Washington. She was on her way to France. The very night that mother was leaving she was going to get up at 3:30 a.m. and take the boat train to France... I'll never forget...she was so excited. Ricki Huston, that very same night had these tickets to a reading. I asked mother did she want to go. She said, "No. I'll stay here with Adam. You go, because I have to get up at 3:30 a.m. because I'm going to France." And she was like a teenager. She was so happy. She said, "I'm going to France." She was going to meet Louise Kent and another friend in Paris. It was 1967. She was sixty. She was so excited. I'll never forget it.

(Primrose begins again.)

That summer we used to go to Primrose Hill. That summer you played with Bobby and the girl from Kansas. She used to dress you up...you used to dress-up and put on plays. It was the most enchanting thing. She was an American girl and she was from Kansas, her name was Dorothy. She used to dress you up in all these costumes and you used to put on plays out in the street. And her parents were so excited that she had an American child to play with.

So everything just seemed...wonderful. We went to Ricki's almost every Sunday; Ricki was a very intuitive person. She knew that when I came to London I only had a little money. She sensed it. She was just like that.

I'm sure she wouldn't have been surprised if I had gone back the next week.

That summer, Ricki had parties in her backyard. Well, it wasn't a backyard. It was a huge garden. That's where her son Tony kept his falcons. And there was a pond. That was the summer that James Fox drove us home in his purple Lotus.

I went to this reading with Ricki. It was on the river. And Ricki said, "Oh, there's Kenneth Tynan." Tynan was the most famous drama critic in the world at the time and his office at the National Theatre was next door to Laurence Olivier's. Also, Kenneth Tynan had pieces in *The New Yorker* constantly.

(Primrose Hill music begins to fade.)

I had never met him, but I had met his wife at Actors Studio once…his ex-wife. She was a playwright. We went over to say hello to him and he said he had never seen *Funnyhouse*, but Ellen Holly, who had a leading role was a friend. He asked what I was doing in London. I told him about the Beatles project and that Victor Spinetti had mentioned it to John Lennon. And *(laughs)* he said, "Larry *[Olivier]* would like that." And he told me to come and see him tomorrow or maybe the day after.

I went by his office at the National and he said he had mentioned the project to Larry and Larry was very interested. Then he said Larry wasn't there right now, but he would like to meet me. And I'm thinking to myself, *(laughs)* Laurence Olivier, Heathcliffe, wants to meet me. Here I am at the National Theatre, in the famous Old Vic, historic famous Old Vic… Laurence Olivier…Vivien Leigh and John Gielgud. I'm sitting in the National Theatre talking to Kenneth Tynan. You know me better than anyone else, Adam. You can imagine already what state I was in.

Tynan said he wanted Victor and me to come by in a few days. Nan played a big role in all this. Nan called up Victor and told him that Kenneth Tynan wanted us to come by his house. Tynan and Olivier ran the National Theatre and running the National Theatre was like running England.

We went by Tynan's house. He lived in a place called Thurloe Square. As you go along, it is right beyond Harrods. He's right on the corner in this beautiful house. So now I'm inside of Kenneth Tynan's house, and all this is happening within the space of a couple of weeks. I'm in Kenneth Tynan's house with Victor Spinetti and we're having tea. We're sitting around having a conversation in his house. And he tells me in this stuttering voice…"I've told Larry about this and we've decided we want to do this. What we'll do first is we'll do a single performance of it, in December." He said, "Larry's very excited about this."

So Victor and I left his house. Now, Victor's been in zillions of plays, but he was excited.

ADAM. **But you didn't have John Lennon's permission at that point?**

ADRIENNE. John Lennon had told Victor that he was interested.

ADAM. **He was interested, but he hadn't given his permission.**

ADRIENNE. He had given his verbal permission. Lennon said he wanted to meet me. But nobody had asked John Lennon to sign anything at that point. I did sign a piece of paper much, much later.

ADAM. **But you hadn't talked to him? This was all based on what Victor had said?**

ADRIENNE. That's right. Totally. Victor went out there. As it turned out, only a handful of people in London could go out to Weybridge. This was a big, big deal. Victor had quite a niche with the Beatles. He had been in both *Help* and *Hard Day's Night*. John Lennon told Victor, "I want to meet Adrienne Kennedy."

Maybe a month or so passed. I'm not sure because

I took you out of school that day. I think it was in September.

(The Beatles theme music begins.)

I kept you out of school so you could meet John Lennon. It was right off Piccadilly Circus. You and I and Victor went there. It was a very plain doorway, almost like a hidden doorway. We walked up these stairs and their studios were in the back of that. There was nothing about it grand or anything.

We walked up these stairs and there was this little room. We walked in and Paul McCartney was sitting on a desk. I'll never forget it. And he looked just like Paul McCartney. He was the only one, to me, who looked exactly like his photos…he had that shiny dark cap of hair. And he turned and smiled. And he was very friendly to Victor. Cordial, friendly, familiar. He had this quality. He just exuded this quality. Victor introduced me to him and he was very cordial, relaxed, very warm. And automatically, he picked you up and put you on his lap and just started to talk to you. Don't ask me what he said to you. I have no idea.

The Beatles liked Black people. They had worked with Mary Wells. They were crazy about Chuck Berry, Little Richard. They had a real regard for Black music. There's been so much more written about it over the last twenty five years.

(The Beatles theme music begins to fade.)

I think the only thing Paul asked me was if I was from New York. And I had a little postcard of Ucello's, Mandolins, I think that's what it's called and I asked him if he would sign it. That's the postcard that was stolen. He looked at it and laughed and signed it.

They talked about John. Paul put you down eventually, but Paul talked to you for quite a while. I don't know what he said. You can't manufacture that, Adam. He had a quality that just filled the room.

I think they said something like, "John is late." So

we waited. I don't know if that was a minute or ten minutes. There were a couple of people in this office doing something. I have no idea what. Finally, Victor said, "I guess we should go."

Paul McCartney said, "He's late. When he comes he's not going to have time to talk to you at all." So we turned to go out of the door and just at that minute, here comes this skinny little guy with all this hair and glasses on, pale skin and wearing an orange poplin jacket.

(The Beatles theme music begins again.)

Victor said, "There's John." And he had the same thing that Paul McCartney had. He just looked at us like we were so special. Victor said, "John, this is Adrienne." I just felt so wonderful. He said something like, "How ya doing?" And I said to him, "This is my son, Adam." And he said, "Hi, my son Adam." And his eyes…he had these eyes that were blazing.

Victor said, "I told Adrienne that you were really interested." John had that really thick Liverpool accent. He said something like, "Yeah. That would be great." He said, "It is really nice to meet you." He had this quality. It was so unprepossessing, so unpretentious. It was like he was glad to meet us, when obviously you would expect it to be the other way around. It was just unbelievable. He was very thin and pale and his hair was hanging down. He looked like a genius. I'll never forget. He turned and looked at us and said something like, "Bye bye." He was nothing like that person that I had seen in the Beatle movies. He was just this thin pale guy with wispy hair and his granny glasses.

We went down the stairs. Victor said John was very excited about this. And I believed he was. I was just so excited. We got in a taxi. I didn't take taxis much in London, because the buses were so wonderful…so was the Underground. And we went to Ricki's and told her that I had met John Lennon. She was so excited. She had never met the Beatles. For some reason, they moved in this tiny circle. So now everybody was excited. I had met John Lennon. I had met Paul McCartney. *(laughs)*

(The Beatles theme music begins to fade.)

I had come to London with less than five hundred dollars in my purse. Now I had a Guggenheim and lived on Chalcot Crescent. I saw Donald Sutherland. David Bailey, the famous fashion photographer, lived around the corner. You loved it. You absolutely loved it. And when Joedy came from Washington with mother...he was just crazy about.

So now I had met Laurence Olivier...no...I hadn't met Laurence Olivier yet. But now I knew Kenneth Tynan and Victor Spinetti. I had met John Lennon and Paul McCartney. I don't want to exaggerate it but we'd met many people. You know that picture where you're playing the game and Joedy's walking on the sidewalk? You both have your vests on. That very Sunday we went to a luncheon at a writer's house in Hampstead. A Sunday literary lunch. We were invited everywhere and we met so many people. Peter Eyre, Elena Bonham Carter, William Gaskill, Edward Bond. We were invited everywhere...John and Margaretta Arden...Adrian Hamilton...Zekes Mokae.

Around November Sheila Scott Wilkinson who had been in one performance of *Funnyhouse* at the Royal Court told me that she had been spending a lot of time with Jimmy Baldwin and his brother David. Baldwin was living somewhere near Chelsea and was feeling a little lonely and wouldn't it be a great idea if we gave a party for him. She mentioned it to Baldwin and he said he would be delighted. Ann and Carlton joined in.

(Ram John Holder West Indian-style music begins to play.)

The party was at our house. We bought cases of wine, cases of liquor, and made huge pans of spinach lasagna.

A friend insisted upon bringing his entire light show. A young musician named Ram John Holder said he'd bring his band. We rented chairs and tables from Harrods. People phoned and asked what to wear. We lit the house with candles. All came. Some even came early. The band came; the light show lit the whole room. People were excited. Then Baldwin came with his English publisher. He talked to people and people talked to him. As he left Baldwin said to me "Think of me as your brother."

(Ram John Holder-style music begins to fade.)

ADAM. You had finished more pages?

ADRIENNE. I had about thirty five pages of the Lennon Play…so where do I go from here? The next time I saw the Beatles? So now we'd met John and Paul. Then we didn't see them anymore. The play was supposed to be around early December, 1967.

(Waterloo Bridge theme music begins.)

I believe Victor and I talked on the phone a couple of times, somewhere between September and December. I know we went once to Kenneth Tynan's office at the National Theatre. It was always for me an incredible experience…you took the Underground to Waterloo Station. Waterloo Station for me was…when I was a kid there was this movie called the Waterloo Bridge. It had Vivien Leigh and Robert Taylor. It was a World War II movie. And they met in the fog in Waterloo Station. And you know that Vivien Leigh had acted at the Old Vic and was Olivier's past wife.

For me to go from Primrose Hill and come up in Waterloo Station was so exciting. You come up and there's the Old Vic. It sits there all by itself. Victor and I went to Tynan's office.

(Waterloo theme music begins to fade.)

I remember he said, "Larry's not here today." Then at some point he said, "I'd like to be the dramaturg on this. We will do the play on Sunday night, in December. And then we're going to put it in our regular season in May." I was so excited. Their posters were all over London. I did end up with a poster. It was blue. I kept it for years. I think I lost it when we moved here.

Victor and I walked over to Harrods. We saw Natalie Wood shopping. We were supposed to start rehearsals. I don't remember the exact date. The rehearsal was going to start in November. We were going to rehearse for three weeks, and John Lennon said he was going to come to the first day of rehearsal.

(An Olivier theme begins to play.)

I arrived at the rehearsal at the Old Vic. I had on a brown woolen dress and brown boots. I'll never forget. And I had this very pretty coat. I'm sitting there at the rehearsal and in walks Laurence Olivier. He came and sat next to me and he was friendly. I just couldn't believe that Laurence Olivier was sitting next to me.

Victor did a scene and I saw that it was very different than what I had written. He came over and said, "Well, you know, I changed it." He said something like, "Ken and I have decided we'll write it with you."

I was dazed. I couldn't believe that I was sitting next to Laurence Olivier. And Laurence Olivier kept smiling at me. Then he left.

Laurence Olivier, I don't know how old he was then. He had gray hair. I guess the closest is like how he look in *Marathon Man*. He had gray hair and he had on a dark suit with a vest.

So then up the stairs came John Lennon. He had on an overcoat. He had on a navy blue overcoat. He looked different. He looked very different. He looked like a Beatle. His hair was combed down. He had bangs, and he had his hands in his pockets. And I don't think he had on his glasses. He looked like John Lennon. He came across the floor and asked how I was doing.

He acknowledged me. He watched a little bit of the rehearsal, and then he said he had to go. He said he was going to come back. Then he went down the stairs and that was it. But he looked like John Lennon.

I was downstairs maybe for an hour later, and at the bottom of the stairs, in a foyer was Laurence Olivier. And I just went up to him and said, "I just can't believe that you're Laurence Olivier." And asked him for his autograph. I was in a daze.

(The Oliver theme music begins to fade.)

Then there was another rehearsal. I don't remember if I went. Victor told me that George Martin wanted to meet me. George Martin wants to take us to lunch. He was the Beatles' arranger. He wanted to do the music. I don't remember going upstairs that day to the rehearsal.

I had lunch with Ringo, John, George Martin and Victor in the pub next to the National Theatre. Victor said, "Ringo might want to do something on it, too. The Beatles might want to work on this." He said something like, "Larry met with John and he's discussed this."

There I was wearing my favorite brown dress. We met them down in the lobby and I walked down to the luncheon with Ringo. These Beatles, they had something. He had these bright eyes. And he wasn't much bigger than I was. We had walked down a few feet and he said something like, "This was a good idea, but it needs a lot of work."

He was very nice…a charm.

We went into the restaurant. I remember all these kids. They were called the Young Vic, were all in there and everyone was staring, of course.

We had this lunch to decide what the play should be. George Martin said he wanted to work on it and he wanted to add some music. He wanted to know what my ideas were. By this time, I was just too over-whelmed. They, George Martin, Ringo, Victor, John, were all sitting as close as we are now. I just retreated. I was just overwhelmed by it. So, I think we walked out to the street and they got in a car and they said good-bye. And I was just...it was too much. I went back to Primrose Hill.

Now I had met Ringo. Somewhere in there, before or after, Victor gave a party for his friend, George Harrison. He said, "I'm going to give a party for the cast of the Young Vic. These are some of the actors that are going to be in it *[the production]* and George is coming." This was an incredible sequence of events. This is maybe October.

Victor lived near Sherlock Holmes...near Baker Street. I arrived. I remember it was cold. It was a small apartment and all the kids from the Young Vic were there, and George and Patti came up the stairs. And, you know, Patti Harrison was one of the most beautiful women in the world. She was devastatingly beautiful. She was in the press every five seconds...British *Vogue*.

They came up the stairs. But they didn't come into the main room. George stayed in the hallway. There was a little room out there. Victor explained that George was shy and he didn't want to come in.

(London Party music begins to play. This music should be a montage of all music and musicians mentioned ear-lier, sounds of parties.)

There was a little room off the foyer. Patti was in the foyer talking to people. So I went out to the little room and George was just standing there kind of off to the side. So I said to myself, "This is crazy. You're not going to say hello to George Harrison?" So I walked up to him and said, "I really love your music." He said, with a tiny voice, "Thank you. Thank you very much." You could tell he meant it. Then he just looked at me and I remember I just backed away from him, because

I couldn't think of anything else to say to him. And he never came in the main room. He just stayed back in this little alcove. It was dark back there. He stayed back in there. Patti was in the foyer. And the way she dressed…I don't know…in Chanel or…there were several London designers who dressed all those people. But she was in British *Vogue* every month practically. So I went and said hello to her and she was very friendly. And she said it was nice to meet me. She's wearing this green chiffon flowing dress and green boots…she had blonde hair with bangs.

And, again, I was just too overwhelmed. I left. It was just too much. And that was the only time I ever met George…his suit was pink. He had crumpled hair. He looked like an intellectual. He was so unpretentious. He didn't seem like his performing persona.

(The Party music begins to fade.)

I don't think I went to any more rehearsals. I'm not sure. Actually, I did go to one more rehearsal that was on the stage at the Old Vic. So again, for me to walk into the Old Vic, and see a play that I had something to do with on the stage…where Olivier and Gielgud and Ralph Richardson and all these people have been, was just too much. John Lennon came to that. Paul McCartney came to that. They had on overcoats. And I talked to Paul McCartney for a second. He said something like, "This is a nice stage." He seemed genuinely excited.

We had one more meeting. We had one more meeting with John Lennon, Victor and Ken Tynan, up in Ken Tynan's office to, again, talk about what was going to happen. And that's when John Lennon was sitting next to me and he said he would be going to India in the spring. He wanted to know when the play was going to be. Tynan told him May or June, and he said he would be back by then. He established that he would not be able to have anything to do with the play but he would be back by then.

So at this meeting it was established that Ken Tynan was going to be the dramaturg; Victor was going to help me write it.

(The Olivier theme music begins to play again. To **ADRI-ENNE,** *Olivier should signify grandeur.)*

Everything seemed to be alright. When we went out of the office Ken Tynan said, "Larry wants to say goodbye to you." *(emotional)* I went down and got in the car and Laurence Olivier came down and said goodbye to me.

ADAM. **Was it like a death wish do you mean? Was he saying like goodbye as in forever?**

ADRIENNE. *(still emotional)* I don't know.

ADAM. **Was he like Don Corleone or what?** *(laughs)*

ADRIENNE. Why do you laugh? I was little Adrienne from Cleveland and Laurence Olivier was coming down to say goodbye to me. That's how the British are. He was very nice.

ADAM. **When you went to rehearsals, obviously the very first rehearsal, you said that you saw it was different.**

ADRIENNE. I saw that Victor…I saw it was different.

(The Olivier theme music goes out.)

ADAM. **Okay. That's what I'm trying to figure out. So when you went to the final rehearsal, the rehearsal that was on the stage, was it even more different?**

ADRIENNE. No. No. No. It was pretty much the same.

ADAM. **Okay. So at that point, half of what you had done…?**

ADRIENNE. Yes. Yes. It was clear Victor wanted to help write it…

ADAM. **So Ken Tynan didn't… ?**

ADRIENNE. No. No. He was just the dramaturg. And somewhere in there, John Lennon…I don't remember…did we do it in person? …There was a little piece of paper that I signed that said that if any royalties resulted from this, John Lennon got sixty percent, I got twenty percent and Victor Spinetti got twenty percent. So everybody was happy, at least as far as I knew.

ADAM. Just from your speculation, do you think that once Victor realized that this was going to happen, do you think he went to John Lennon and said would it be okay if I helped write this?

ADRIENNE. I don't know, at the rehearsal he said, "I'm help-ing. I'm helping to write this." It seemed natural…that we'd be co-authors…

You laughed about Olivier. You see, I'm learning as I tell you this. Laurence Olivier was mother's favorite actor. She was crazy about him. And I was crazy about him. I love his Heathcliffe immensely, his *Hamlet.* So then, it seems to me that we had one more meeting at the National. Because that's the time John Lennon took Victor and me home in his car. He had this big black car and this chauffeur. John asked me if I wanted to play with the car telephone. He said you can talk to anybody in the world.

ADAM. He had a telephone in the car?

ADRIENNE. Yeah. You see, I can't explain how he was. There was nothing about him that was pompous. He said, "Do you want to play with the telephone?" I remember saying no.

He said we could all go out to lunch, but first he had to make a stop at someone's house. He wanted to see if anyone was home. He said, "I'll see if they're home. If they're not home, we can all go out to lunch." So he went up a flight of stone stairs and he came back. It was near Belgrave Square. He said they were home and he told his chauffeur to take us where we wanted to go.

So Victor and I were in a car with John Lennon's chauf-feur. John always said things like "bye bye" or "toodle loo." He used toodle loo a lot. He said, "Toodle loo." And I hadn't heard toodle loo since my summers in

Georgia. You know so many Georgia expressions were British expressions.

The chauffeur took Victor home first, because Victor was near Baker Street. Then the chauffeur took me home and asked me for a date. *(laughs)* He said, "Would you like to go out tonight?" *(still laughing).* He was a huge guy. He looked to be Mediterranean, like a big boxer.

Anyway, I don't want to get into analyzing it. But John Lennon made it very clear that he was very happy that he was going to have a play at the National Theatre based on his works. I remember he said in the office, "Maybe it will be running when I'm thirty." He actually said that.

ADAM. How old was he?

ADRIENNE. Well, he was born in 1940, and that was 1967. So how old would that make him?

ADAM. Twenty seven.

ADRIENNE. He actually said that. He said, "Maybe it will be running when I'm thirty." And he laughed. That was the time when we were in Ken Tynan's office. And he had this tiny little laugh. He had a little high-pitched laugh.

For the Sunday evening, I had a special coat made. There was a young tailor. He used to always talk to me in Primrose Hill. He was about twenty four years old. He and his wife were both designers and they had a little dressmaking shop right there on Regents Park Road…it was a charming little dress making shop.

He was interested in my coats. He would say he could tell I was an American. He said, "Where did you buy that coat?" I had a gray coat. I bought it at Saks. He said it was a very pretty coat, based on the lines of Givenchy. And it was, because I used to try to…wear imitation Givenchy.

He made this coat out of a tapestry and a skirt and a

dark blue blouse. I kept it until I moved off of 79th Street. *[In New York]* I wore it for years and years and years. When you went away to college, I lost track of it.

That night Victor told me he would be talking to the actors, running them through their final paces and I was supposed to have dinner with Laurence Olivier, Kenneth Tynan and Penelope and John Mortimer. John Mortimer, a writer, who wrote *Rumpole*, was a famous lawyer also. And his wife was a screenwriter. She wrote this wonderful screenplay called *Pumpkin Eater*. I was supposed to have dinner with the Mortimers and Olivier and Tynan. So that's what I did.

I can see now…I didn't really understand this…*(emotional)* It's Olivier that makes me cry…I had dinner with Laurence Olivier sitting right next to me in a restaurant right next to the Old Vic. *(wistful)* And I was just…

ADAM. So, in retrospect you said you were overwhelmed. Were you talking?

ADRIENNE. I was barely talking. Adam.

ADAM. I mean were you holding full-fledged conversations with these people?

ADRIENNE. No! I wasn't holding full-fledged conversations. I think they were saying things like, "We hope it goes well tonight."

… Adam, I was totally…fixed…on the fact that Laurence Olivier was sitting next to me. That's all I could think of…I said out loud…without meaning to, "I can't believe you're Laurence Olivier."…I could barely see the others…I only knew his arm was near mine. And that he glanced at me. He had on a jacket…a brownish tweed.

I think they had already decided that they were going to dump me. By the time of this dinner, they had decided that John Lennon was the author. And Victor was the director. And I understand later, from Victor, that Olivier had met with John Lennon maybe once or twice.

ADAM. Had they decided that they would keep your name on it?

ADRIENNE. They knew already that they wanted John Lennon to be the author. I don't know how to spell it out...you know, that's common in theatre, movies too... you sort of keep somebody's name on it...but they had already decided that John Lennon was to be the author. They were going to deal with John Lennon from then on. John Lennon was going to be the person they would deal with. I don't know how else to say it. They would keep my name somewhere there. They had already made up their minds about that.

So we had this dinner...Adam, you asked was I talking. I was considerably quiet in those days. I was quiet with everyone. I've talked more in the last twenty years than I've ever talked. I was a quiet person. So if I'm sitting eating dinner, whether it is Laurence Olivier or whoever, I'm not saying all that much. I was quiet. I've gotten more talkative...I mean, you're not a good person to judge this...I can hold casual conversations with people much better in the last twenty years as I've gotten older. I wasn't talking. But I did blurt out that one thing.

As I recall, Kenneth Tynan was very talkative. I would imagine...I don't remember...He would just be saying like, "so and so and so... " And Olivier would just look at me. I don't know why. But he would just look at me.

As we walked down the street to go back to the theatre, I'll never forget it, Sean Connery came along the street with Diane Cielento. And I remember Kenneth Tynan saying, "There's Sean Connery." Kenneth Tynan said something like, "John couldn't come to the dinner, but John's coming tonight."

(Music plays, signifying the entrance into the theatre.)

As we went into the theatre Kenneth Tynan disappeared…and the Mortimers disappeared…Laurence Olivier said to me, "We're going to sit together."

To get into the theatre, we had had to pass by all these people. That's the first time this ever happened. I was on the red carpet. There were people behind velvet ropes. I'll never forget. Ann was behind the ropes, Ann Colcord. There were people behind the ropes. That's never happened, before or since. The ropes ran all the way upstairs. People were waiting to see Laurence Olivier and to see the Beatles. Laurence Olivier was holding my arm. I wish I had a picture of it. My friend Ann called out my name. Laurence Olivier led me to my seat. When the play started…I think I told you that…he took my hand.

Well you see, Adam. You can laugh if you want to… Adrienne from Cleveland…I was out of it. I could have had cut my head off…I was sitting next to Laurence Olivier…Laurence Olivier. There were people behind these gold ropes. There's my best friend in London behind a gold rope waving at me.

(The music fades.)

They had decided that I was expendable. And they were going to do it as gracefully as possible. I think somebody told me much later, Mike Weller, an American playwright. He said, "You weren't a major American writer. You weren't Norman Mailer. Yes. You had an OBIE, but they felt that they could gracefully do it."

John came in at the very end. That's when I really got the first sense that he was a Beatle. Because at the very end, right before the lights went down, he ran in with his wife, Cynthia. He ran in and he sat down in front. And all these people started whispering, "There's John Lennon. There's John Lennon." And all these celebrities were there. I don't know who they were. Sean Connery…I mean all these celebrities came to see this.

It was celebrities, celebrities, celebrities. All I knew was Laurence Olivier was holding my hand and he would look at me and smile.

When it was over, I don't remember anything about the play really, we went into the aisle, and walked down to the front. Kenneth Tynan was standing there. He said, "John left." Laurence Olivier turned and looked at me and said goodnight.

As I'm telling you this, it is very clear that Laurence Olivier was the most important person in this thing for me. He looked at me and he smiled and said goodnight. And I think Kenneth Tynan said, "Larry has to go back to the country," or something like that. And Tynan said, "Would you like to have dinner with us?"

But I was having dinner with the Hustons. They took me to a famous Italian restaurant. I don't know the name of it. I think a lot of movie stars went there.

It was Ricki, Tony, Anjelica. I was excited. I was working with the Beatles. There was going to be a play by the end of May or beginning of June…on the stage at the National Theatre. The cast would be the Young Vic.

ADAM. Were there reviews of this performance?

ADRIENNE. I don't know. The next morning I didn't hear from Victor. Victor used to call me up sometimes in the morning. I didn't hear from him and I was surprised I didn't hear from him. I remember exactly where I was sitting in the bedroom. The phone was downstairs in the bedroom. So I called him up at about ten or eleven o'clock.

He said, "I have something to tell you. John wants to be the author of this play. You'll have to discuss it with Tynan. Larry has met with him, and John wants to be the author. That's all I know. You'll have to discuss it with Ken." And then he said, "What do you know about a Liverpool boy's childhood?"

I called Ken Tynan. He said, "I'm working on a deadline now. I can't talk to you." He said, "It has all been settled. John's going to work on this. It has all been settled." And he hung up. So there I was. I was Adrienne Kennedy again.

I was crying…you know Joe Chaikin. Joe had been in London doing *American, Hurrah*. And he had taken me over to Adrian Mitchell's house in Hampstead. Adrian, a very well known poet, had worked on *Marat Sade*. He and his wife and children lived near Nan Lanier.

I called him. I asked Adrian what I could do. He said, "I don't know. I don't know what you can do. You're not a member of any British writer's group. You don't have any recourse." He said he would ask John Mortimer what I should do. He said he would call me right back, and he did. He said, "I talked to John Mortimer and he said you really don't have much recourse. You did sign a paper for the Sunday night. But the contract you signed was only for the Sunday night.

Then Adrian called another friend. I think he wrote *Bedazzled* and was a part of *Beyond the Fringe*. Adrian said his friend lived near John Lennon in Weybridge. And maybe he could go over and talk to John and find out what happened. So Adrian called his friend and he went to see John.

Adrian called me back later that day. He said, "John's going to call you." The phone rang soon after. He said, "Adrienne, this is John. What's it all about?" And I told him they were going to kick me out of the project. I'll never forget. There was a silence. He said something like, "I'm sorry to hear that." I said, "They told me that you wanted to write it." He said, "I don't want to write it. I'm going to India next week, and I'm not coming back until May." He said, "I'm sorry to hear this." He was silent for a while then he said, "Why don't we all meet in my office at Apple on Monday?" He said, "I'll be in my office at Apple on Monday afternoon. You and Victor come by and we'll straighten all this out." I'll never forget. He said, "We'll clear the air." Then he said, "Toodle loo."

Victor called me up and said that John said we're supposed to meet at Apple. He said, "I'll meet you out in front." I think Apple was somewhere over there by Savile Row.

I met Victor out in front of Apple. You could tell Victor was very angry. We went up in the elevator and he said, "I don't know what you're doing." We got off the elevator. It was a crowded room. You could tell they were the Beatles. The room was just loaded with people doing things, lots of activity. Secretaries were just running around, lots of people. Apple was their headquarters.

A secretary told us that John would be right with us. A split second later, John comes out of this room. He looked at me and said, "We're going to straighten this out." He looked like he did the first time I met him. He had on his granny glasses. He didn't look like a Beatle. He did have these different personas. His hair was disheveled. He looked like a mad genius.

He led us into this little office, this tiny office. It was empty except for a desk and a couple of chairs. He said, "Victor, I don't want Adrienne Kennedy kicked out of this project. And I'm going to call up Ken Tynan while she's sitting here." He picked up the phone. He said, "I've told Tynan I was going to call him. I told him we were meeting."

He called up Ken Tynan. He said, "I want you to know that Adrienne Kennedy is here. Victor is here. I don't want her kicked out of this project. I'm going to India next week. I don't have time and I don't want to write it."

That went on for maybe three minutes. He walked us out to the lobby and said goodbye. I'll never forget how he looked. He looked like someone deep in another domain.

Victor and I went down in the elevator. Victor said

goodbye. John was going to India for all those months. That was maybe December. So I kind of put it in the back of my mind. I knew we wouldn't be starting rehearsals until May. I thought it was all settled. In January, I looked forward to going to Paris to see *Funnyhouse of a Negro* at the Petit Odeon, directed by the great Jean Marie Serreau, which we did.

I continued corresponding with Joe Papp about my play *Cities in Bezique* being at The Public in its second season.

The Beatles went to India. They were all over the papers. There was something called the *Daily Express.* I don't know when it was. Maybe it was in April. I felt secure. I got another Rockefeller grant thanks to Henry Romney. Joe was still sending me alimony. I decided I would try to stick it out in London maybe another six months.

Ricki called me to have lunch. Then she asked me, "Why aren't you at the rehearsals?" She said, "The rehearsals of the *Lennon Play.*"

Knowing Ricki, that's why she invited me to lunch, to tell me. She said, "Well they've been rehearsing the *Lennon Play* for three weeks. My friend told me."

I talked to Adrian once more. He said there was nothing I could do. He said, "You don't belong to any British organization that can protect you. There's nothing you can do." And he encouraged me to let go of it. He's a wonderful person. He said, "Let go of it. They are tough guys." He knew them all well, so I just let go of it.

Elena Bonham Carter was a friend of mine. She was close friends with the woman who produced *Funnyhouse* in Boston, named Stephanie Sills. Stephanie had taken me over there when she had come to London.

Elena wanted to help. She thought I had such a very wonderful London life. We used to go over there.

Her home on West Heath with a circular drive had a romantic setting...paintings of ships...a tennis court. She got her lawyer. They were called Crawley and De Reya. I still have their letterhead somewhere. They were lawyers to royalty.

She asked him could he do anything. He looked into it and told her that there was nothing he could do.

So I decided to let go of it. They called me a few days before the play opened in June. A woman said, "Laurence Olivier and Ken Tynan would like to invite you to the opening of *The Lennon Play.*" I couldn't believe it. "There'll be four tickets for you." On the same day someone else from the National called me and said they wanted me to know that they were going to put my name on the program and poster. I did not go to the play.

My mother sent me a dozen red roses on opening night. I had never told her that I had lost the project. She sent them to the National Theatre, London, England. They were delivered to me on Chalcot Crescent the next day.

I think the play closed quickly. Someone sent me the blue National Theatre poster.

And Joedy who loved the Beatles so much sent me a telegram from Sierra Leone. Even though he and Joe knew I had lost the project, they had an article about it put in the paper in Sierra Leone. Remember that little blue book, *In His Own Write*, had been Joedy's.

We were in London another fourteen months only briefly returning to New York for the opening of *Cities in Bezique* at the Public Theater.

Bill Gaskill was the head of the Royal Court. He gave teas. I believe they were on Tuesday afternoons. People I saw at those teas were John Osborne, Lord Snowdon, Jane Asher and Edward Bond. One of the best productions I ever saw there was *The Three Sisters* with

Marianne Faithfull and *Early Morning* by Edward Bond with Peter Eyre. The Royal Court commissioned me to write my play *Sun* for their new theatre called Upstairs at the Court.

(Music begins to play. This music should convey **ADRIENNE***'s release from London.)*

Ricki Huston was killed in an automobile accident early 1969. Late summer I packed our bags and came home. We arrived just as the Manson Murders occurred.

ADAM. And what is your reaction today?

ADRIENNE. I told it to you as honestly as I could…my search for fame and fortune.

End

Also by
Adrienne Kennedy...

Funnyhouse of a Negro

Ohio State Murders

The Owl Answers

Please visit our website **samuelfrench.com** for complete
descriptions and licensing information

OTHER TITLES AVAILABLE FROM SAMUEL FRENCH

MAURITIUS
Theresa Rebeck

Comedy / 3m, 2f / Interior

Stamp collecting is far more risky than you think. After their mother's death, two estranged half-sisters discover a book of rare stamps that may include the crown jewel for collectors. One sister tries to collect on the windfall, while the other resists for sentimental reasons. In this gripping tale, a seemingly simple sale becomes dangerous when three seedy, high-stakes collectors enter the sisters' world, willing to do anything to claim the rare find as their own.

"(Theresa Rebeck's) belated Broadway bow, the only original play by a woman to have its debut on Broadway this fall."
- Robert Simonson, *New York Times*

"*Mauritius* caters efficiently to a hunger that Broadway hasn't been gratifying in recent years. That's the corkscrew-twist drama of suspense… she has strewn her script with a multitude of mysteries."
- Ben Brantley, *New York Times*

"Theresa Rebeck is a slick playwright… Her scenes have a crisp shape, her dialogue pops, her characters swagger through an array of showy emotion, and she knows how to give a plot a cunning twist."
- John Lahr, *The New Yorker*